Hasan

CHAPTERS

DOG MAN
LORD OF THE FLEAS

WRITTEN AND ILLUSTRATED BY DAV PILKEY
AS GEORGE BEARD AND HAROLD HUTCHINS
WITH COLOR BY JOSE GARIBALDI

AN IMPRINT OF
SCHOLASTIC

THANK YOU TO A DEAR FRIEND, RACHEL "RAY RAY" COUN, WHO WAS THERE FROM THE START

Library of Congress Control Number 2017963497

978-0-545-93517-3 (POB)
978-1-338-29091-2 (Library)

10 9 8 7 6 5 4 3 2 1 18 19 20 21 22

Printed in China 62
First edition, September 2018

Edited by Anamika Bhatnagar
Book design by Dav Pilkey and Phil Falco
Color by Jose Garibaldi
Creative Director: David Saylor

DOG MAN

Behind the Epicness!

Yo, Homies, It's George and Harold again!

What up, dogs?

We're in 5th grade now, which means we're totally mature.

And deep!

I think I might grow a moustache!

me too!

Our new teacher makes us read CLASSIC LITERATURE!
Lord of the Flies
William Golding

Fortunately, the books have all been pretty good.
Lord of The
Lord of The

Don't you agree, Harold?
Well, um...

I didn't really finish Lord of the Flies.

WHAT?

But don't worry! I've seen all the movies a bunch of times!!!

ALL WHAT movies?
You know: "my Precious!"

LORD OF THE FLIES is **NOT** THE SAME thing as LORD OF THE RINGS!!!

It's a story of savagery...

OUR STORY THUS FAR...

by George and Harold

One time there was a cop and a police dog...

...Who got hurt in an explosion.

KA-BLAMMERS

When they got to the hospital, the doctor had sad news:

But just when everything seemed hopeless, the nurse Lady got an idea.

Let's sew the dog's head onto the cop's body!

OK, nurse Lady!

So they did.

And soon, a new crime-fighting sensation was unLeashed.

HOORAY FOR DOG MAN!

Along the way, Dog Man has made some very awesome friends.
Zuzu: World's Greatest Poodle
Sarah Hatoff: World's Great-est reporter
Chief: World's Greatest Chief
Our Hero
chief

And one supa evil enemy!

WANTED
for being a jerk

PETEY
World's most evilest cat

Recently, Petey tried to clone himself...
I'll make a big, evil villain, Just Like me!
DNA
START

...but instead, he got a tiny, cute kitten who was nothing like him.
Papa!
Li'L Petey: world's Greatest kitty

Li'l Petey's Life started out Sad...
Free Kitty

...but it wasn't sad for long.
Free kitty
DoG Man

Now Li'l Petey has a family.
Pat Pat Pat
Kiss kiss kiss
80-HD: world's Greatest Robot buddy

And that is a good place to start.
DoG Man

Chapter 1

A Visit from Kitty Protective Services

By George and Harold

One morning at Dog Man's house...
Buzz
Buzz
Buzz
clank
clank
clank
DOG MAN

...Li'l Petey and 80-HD were hard at work.
Buzz
Buzz
Buzz
clank
clank
clank

Well, I'm all done reprogramming the Dogmobile!

Now it's super easy to control!

How's the hydraulic Roof Ramp coming along?

CLAP CLAP

RRRRR

RRR

RRRRRR
DOG MAN

Awesome!!!
Dog Man
CLUNK!

I can't wait until Dog Man sees it!

Grand Ballroom
DING

Good Morning, Dog Man!!!

Look what me and 80-HD did!

We transformed the Grand Ballroom into the coolest clubhouse EVER!!!

Us three are going to be in a club, ok?

We'll call ourselves the SUPA BuddieS!

Most of the time, we'll just be our regular selves...
Flop Flip

...But when danger rears its ugly head...

...We'll be super-heroes!!!

Look—I even made a cape for 80-HD!

LD

And I made him a Flip-O-Rama mask!

Ya just tape it here...
...and now he's **brave**, see?
But if you flip it up...
...He's **Happy**!
He looks so different. You can't even tell it's him!!!
So I'll be **Cat Kid**, You can be **The Bark Knight**...
FLIP FLOP FLIP

...And 80-HD will be Lightning Dude!
FLOP FLIP FLOP FLIP
This is gonna be SWEEEEET!
OH. It's time for Breakfast!
Cat food and cream for me...
...Dog Food and gravy for you...
...And nuts and bolts and motor oil for 80-HD!
Grape nuts + Bolts
OIL

Hey! I know...

...Let's all eat in FLIP-O-Rama!

It's an important part of this nutritious breakfast!!!

INTRODUCING
FLIP

STEP 1.

First, Place your Left hand inside the dotted Lines marked "Left hand here." HoLd The book open FLAT!

STEP 2:

Grasp the right-hand Page with your Thumb and index finger (inside the dotted Lines marked "Right Thumb Here").

STEP 3:

Now QUICKLY flip the right-hand page back and forth until the Picture appears to be Animated.

(For extra fun, try adding your own sound-effects!)

Remember,

while you are flipping, be sure you can see the image on page 23 **AND** the image on page 25.

If you flip quickly, the two pictures will start to look like one **ANIMATED** cartoon!

Don't forget to add your own sound-effects!

Left hand here.

Right
Thumb
here.

grape
nuts
+
bolts

DiNG DoNG
Doorbell!

RUFF! RUFF! RUFF!
RUFF! RUFF! RUFF!
FLIP
FLOP

RUFF! RUFF!
Stairs
RUFF! RUFF! RUFF!
FLIP
FLOP

Flop
Flip
Flop
Flip
Flop
FLIP
Ruff
RUFF
Ruff
RUFF
RUFF
RUFF

RUFF RUFF RUFF
RUFF RUFF RUFF
FLIP FLOP FLIP

RUFF RUFF RUFF
DOG MAN

RUFF RUFF RUFF
RUFF
RUFF
RUFF
FLIP FLOP

Don't You Bark AT ME!!
RUFF

AND YOU STOP BARKING, TOO!!!

That's BETTER!!!
DOG MAN

I was sent here by Kitty Protective services...

Apparently, you've got a Kitten who Should be in SchooL!

Come with me, young man!

GRRRRRRR

Don't You DARE GrowL At ME!!!

Kittens HAVE To Go to school!!! IT's the LAW!!!

Do you WANT to Pay a Fine?

Do You WANT to GO TO JAIL?

Do You want to LOSE CUSTODY?

It's Okay, Dog Man!

I'll go to School...

...and we can play together when I get back, okay?

Bye, Dog Man!
Bye, 80-HD!

Costumes
LD

STUFF
STUFF
STUFF
costumes

Meanwhile...
Well, hello there, little fella.
Hi, Papa!

Ha-Ha! I think you've confused me with someone else!
No I haven't!

I'm a kindly old social worker!!!
No you're not.

I only care about your best interests!!!
No you don't.

Look, kid, I'm NOT who you THINK I Am!
Yes you are!

I AM NOT Your PAPA!!!
Yes you are.

NO I'm NOT!
Yes you are!

AM NOT!!!
Are too!

AM NOT!
Are too!

AM NOT!
Are too!

I AM NOT!!!
Ya Are too!

POP
PUNT
ZIP
Shuffle
shuffle
NGYA!

I knew you were my Papa!

Look, Kid — I'm NOT your Papa! You're MY CLONE!!!

CLONES DON'T HAVE PAPAS!!!
Well I do!

Look--- I have HAD IT WITH YOU!

It's Not even NOON, And you're ALREADY DRIVING ME NUTS!
YAY!

Hey, where's the School at, Papa?

We're not going to School. We're getting outta Town!
Why?

Because you're in terrible DANGER!
Why?

I'm not gonna tell you!
Why?

Because every time I tell a Story, you always interrupt me, like, a Thousand Times!
Why?

Because You're A PEST!!!
Why?

SiT DOWN!!!
why?

Because we need to talk!
why?

Look --- it's **very irritating** when you
Hey Papa, you got weird hairs in your nose!

YOU JUST INTERRU
I won't interrupt anymore. I'll be good.

ALRight, because what I'm about to tell you is
Hey Papa, is this story gonna be boring?

NO!

Okay. You may continue.

Well, it All started this morning when I was in
Hey Papa! Do y'wanna hear a joke?

I AM GOING TO FINISH TELLING MY STORY...

...AND YOU ARE GOING TO LISTEN QUIETLY WITH NO INTERRUPTIONS!!!
Okay.

CHAPTER 2

PETEY'S STORY

(WITH MANY INTERRUPTIONS)

Alright, listen carefully...
This whole mess started today at sunrise.
cat Jail
I was in my Jail cell minding my own business...
...when the guard comes in and starts messin' with me.
Yoo-Hoo!!! Petey!
What'cha doin'?
nothin'

Hey! You're not building a giant Robot, are you?
NO.
Oh good! That's a relief!
Well, come with me. It's Time for your appointment.
What appointment?
You have to see the Psychiatrist.
I ain't seein' no head shrinker!

Sorry, Petey. The Judge says ya have to.
RATS!
So anyway...
Petey, meet Dr. Katz.
It's a pleasure to meet you, Petey.
Yeah, I know!
Hey Papa, that guy looks like the costume you wore.
JUST PAY ATTENTION!!! It'll all make sense soon!
OK.
So Anyway...
Dr. Katz

My records show that you've been locked up here seven times...
... and you've escaped SIX times!
Yeah, well--- it's been a busy week!
Petey, we need to get to the ROOT of your problems!

Hey Papa, how come I'm wearing a hat?

That's Not **YOU**! That's **ME** when I was a Kitten!

Oh.

So anyway, I used to be an **AWESOME** scout!
SCOUT'S GUIDE TO GOOD Behavior
CS
Here's another badge for you, Petey!
Sweeeet!
I was known far and wide for my good deeds and merit badges!
But it all ended one day when we went to play miniature golf.
5
PUTT PUTT ISLAND

You kids play nice! I'm gonna go get some coffee!
OK.
Everything started out great...
...but then a terrible storm arose.
PUT
PUT
ISLA
The whole place began to flood.
4
We hid on a tiny boat.

4
CS
But the water rose higher and higher...
...and soon we were washed away.
The storm raged for weeks and weeks.
Finally, we landed on a deserted island.

Well, Petey, What do we do now???
We must use our Scout Skills to Survive.
We can hunt for food...
...and we can use Piggy's glasses...
My specs!
...To light campfires and Stuff!
Together, we can build up a utopia...

...based on hard work, respect, and civility.
What do you say, fellas?
We'll try our best, Petey!
Nine Minutes Later...
ATTACK!!!

Crunky the Ape and Bub the crocodiLe had their own agenda.
CS
CS
And Soon...
CS
CS
...A pointy blade was before us...
CS
CS
... and hungry Sharks with razor-Sharp teeth were below us.
And Then
Hey Papa, Knock-Knock!

ARE YOU EVEN LISTENING?

You're s'posed to say "who's there?"

C'mon, Papa. It's a good one!

WHO'S There?

Ummm...

Uhhh...

A flower!

A flower who?

A flower pooped on your head!

HA HA
HA
HA Ha
HA
Ha Ha

Ha Ha
Ha HA
Ha
Ha HA
HA
Ha

HA HA
Ha
Ha Ha
Ha HA
Ha
Ha HA
Ha

THAT DOESN'T EVEN MAKE SENSE!
Ha Ha
Ha

LOOK, Kid... This is SERIOUS!!!
Ha Ha
HA Ha
Ha
Ha

I'm POURING MY HEART out to YOU!
HA Ha HA
HA Ha
Ha

YOU NEED to PAY ATTENTION!!!
OK, OK.

So ANYWAY...

There we were, Piggy and me...
...at the brink of DEATH...
MY SPECS!
...losing the battle between civilization and savagery.
CRUNCH
CRUNCH
When suddenly...
HEY!
PUTT-PUTT ISLAND
8

WHAT Are You Kids DoinG?
CS
I WAS GONE For TEN MinuTES...
CS
...AND You've Regressed into MANiACS!
What are You, a Bunch of ANiMALS??
When I find out who was responsible...

Petey did it!
CS
CS
CS
CS
CS

Wait---So that whole Part about the Flood and the island was all make-believe?

Well, yeah---but that's not the Point!

The Point is, I WAS BETRAYED!
And then he started a Fire!
Then he fed my specs to the SHARKS!
We tried to STOP him!!!
CS
CS
CS
CS

In the end, I got kicked out of the Critter Scouts!
CS
All my good deeds were erased!
CS
All my virtuous hard work meant nothing...
...Life ... was... pointless.
I guess things were never the same after that, Doc.
And what about Piggy and Crunky and Bub?

Oh, I got my revenge against those guys!!!
How?
I just made a few phone calls to the right people.
Hello, Animal Rights Union?
Soon their whole organization was flooded with anti-discrimination lawsuits.
CRITTER SCOUTS UNFAIR to CATS
CATS AGAINST CRITTER SCOUTS
CRITTER SCOUTS HURT MY "Feelines"
SCOUTS OUT!
CATS Are People, Too!!!
The Critter Scouts was shut down within a **week**!!!
What happened to Piggy, Crunky, and Bub?
Who cares?

I'LL TELL YOU WHAT HAPPENED!
POP
PIGGY?
We Lost OUR badges, too!!!
OUR Lives became pointless as well...
ZZZiP
...And We began Planning our OWN Revenge...

AGAiNST YOU!!!

HAW HAW
HAW HAW

CRUNKY and Bub are waiting outside!!!

Now That we've got YOU, we're gonna destroy Someone YOU LOVE!

YOUR LITTLE CLONE!

Wait--- you Love me?

JUST PAY ATTENTION!
Okay.

So Anyway...

... Then, we're gonna Take over the world in our GIANT ROBO-BRONTOSAURUS!!!
It's Parked outside!!!

HAW HAW HAW HAW HAW

HAW HAW HAW HAW HAW

HAW HAW
HAW HAW
HAW HAW
HAW HAW
HAW
HAW
HAW
HAW
HAW
HAW
HAW HAW HAW
HAW HAW HAW

HAW HAW HAW
ZIP!
HAW HAW HAW
Oh, Guard!
Yes, Doctor?
An evil pig just broke in...
... And Swallowed Petey!!!
I'LL SAVE YA, Petey!!!
HAW HAW

Hold on, Petey!
I'm Comin' For YA!
OH, CRUNKY! OH, Bub!
Help is on the way!
Yeah, boss?
HELP THAT GUARD!
Okay, boss!

Psychiatry center
SLAM
LOCK
Lemme at him!
We're Helping!!!
Bye, Dr. Katz!
So Long, Sucka!
HAW HAW!
Cat Jail

So THAT'S why I came to get you...

...And THAT'S why we need to get as far away from here as possible.

But Papa, if the bad guys got locked up, why are we running?

Because they'll probably ESCAPE!

But how could they escape from a maximum security prison?

Who knows? Maybe something DUMB will happen!

Chapter 3

Something Dumb Happens!

by George Beard and Harold Hutchins

Meanwhile...
COPS
Ring-Ring

Hello?
Chief

Help! There's been a JaiL escape!!!
chief

Where?
chief
at the JaiL.
Oh!

I'll put my best man on it!!!!!!!
chief

Oh, DOG MAN!
chief

Dog Man is Late for work again, Chief!
chief

Beep
Beep
Beep
Beep
Beep
chief

DOG MAN! We Need your help!
chief

Meet US AT The JAIL in Ten Minutes!

AND DON'T Get DISTRACTED!!!

RUFF RUFF
RUFF

RUFF
RUFF RUFF
RUFF

Meanwhile...
wee-ooo-wee-ooo-wee-

Cat
JaiL
SCREEEEEECh!

OH, NOOOO!
What's wrong, Milly?
chief

It's A giant ROBO-BRONTOSAURUS!!!
This is worse Than I expected!

Where is Dog Man? He should be here by now!
chief

He's Probably off chasing Squirrels again!
chief

We're gonna have to go in without him!
chief

FREEZE SUCKAS!
chief
CRASH

...Where Chief and Milly have just caught three crooks!

Chief

Left hand here.

CHIEF

CHIEF

Right
Thumb
here.

chief

Left hand here.

Encyclopedia Obsoletica

chief
DicTionery

Right Thumb here.

chief

Well, congratulations on capturing the crooks!!!
Thanks. I only wish Dog Man was here.
chief

Yeah, where IS Dog Man?
I'm gonna find out!
chief
Beep Beep Beep

RUFF
RUFF
RUFF
♪ RING-RING-RING ♪

DOG MAN---
WHERE ARE YOU?

I can't wait to show him what we did!!!
chief

Here He comes now!!!
chief

Oh boy, This is gonna be **GREAT!**
Cat Jail

NO--- WAIT!!
chief

NOOOO!
chief

STOP
CUT IT OUT
MBLFFF
QUIT IT!
ENOUGH!
BAD DOGGY

WHAT is Your MAJOR MALfunction?

CRASH!
chief

OH, NO! They're GetTing AWAY!

Cat JaiL

chief

chief

Come on, Zuzu! Let's follow them!
chief

DOG MAN, Those Guys escaped because of YOU!!!
chief

GO HOME!
chief

But Chief –
Sorry, Milly. He's gotta Learn his Lesson!
chief

...And We've gotta catch those crooks Again!
chief

Chapter 4

Revenge of the Fleas!

by George and Harold

Meanwhile...
Hey Papa! Knock-Knock!

WOULD YOU CUT THAT OUT?!!?
You're s'posed to say "Who's there?"

C'mon, Papa! It's a really awesome one this time!

Who's There?

Ummmm...

Uhhhhh...

A Sidewalk.

A Sidewalk who?

A Sidewalk pooped on your head!

Ha
Ha Ha Ha
Ha
Ha Ha

THAT'S NOT HOW KNOCK-KNOCK JOKES WORK!

Ha Ha Ha Ha Ha Ha

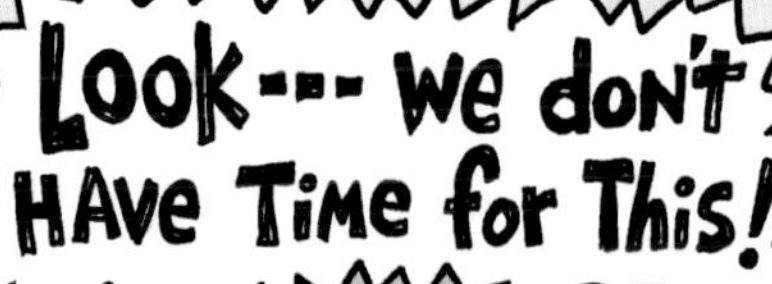

NO!!!
Aw, come on!

It's a super-dooper good one!

C'mon---Knock-Knock!
Knock-Knock, Papa!

WHO's There?

A biG Robot bronto-Saurus!

AAAAH!
chief

Papa! You're s'posed to say "a big Robot brontosaurus who?"
This is Sarah Hatoff with a breaking news update!

A big Robot bronto-saurus is attacking...

...and the good guys are in hot pursuit!
chief

Now it's time for my exclusive interview with the crooks!!!
CHIEF

We're not crooks! We're megalomaniacs!

I am Piggy, Leader of the FLEAS!!!
The FLEAS?

It's an acronym for Fuzzy Little Evil Animal Squad!

But Boss, I'm not Fuzzy.
And I'm not Little.

Left hand here.

Right Thumb here.

chief
chief

chief

So, ya think you're TOUGH, do ya? Well, take THIS!!!
chief
CLANK!
chief
HEEELP!!!
chief
HAW
HAW HAW
HAW
SEWER
It looks like you've reached the end, Petey!

SEWER
WHAM!
Smoosh
Smoosh
Smoosh
Hey! Where'd they go???
SEWER
SEWER
Sniff
Sniff
I bet They escaped down that sewer!!!

Hey Papa,
What?

Knock-Knock!

This is not the time or the place for that!

No, seriously! This is the best one ever!
ALRight, who's There?

Ummm...

A Ladder Pooped on your head.

Ha
Ha Ha
Ha Ha
Ha

A Ladder who?

A Ladder.

Uhhh...

Look---That's not how those Jokes are supposed to go.
Ha Ha Ha Ha Ha
Knock-Knock Jokes have a very specific structure!
Ha Ha Ha
They're based on switching expectations!
I'll give you an example:
Knock-Knock!
Who's There?

Don't ya get it?
But you're not in a bathtub!
Dwayne the bathtub! I'm Dwowning!
Dwayne
Dwayne who?

That's NOT the point!

The point is, you were expecting Someone named "Dwayne."
CaT JaiL

But I Switched it around!

That's why it's funny!

IT Woulda been funnier if the bathtub pooped on your head!

WHAT IS IT WITH YOU AND POOP?
Ha Ha Ha

Look, you can't tell the same Joke...

...over and over...

...and expect it to still be funny!

You can't do the same things...

...again and again...

...and expect to get a Laugh!

Ya gotta avoid repetition...

... Shun redundancy...
Cat Jail

...eschew reiteration...
Cat Jail

...resist recapitulation...
Cat Jail

...And also, stop telling the same Joke over and over!

Chapter 5

A Buncha Stuff That Happened Next

DOG
Man

DOG
Man

Condensed
DOG
FOOD

Breaking NEWS

We now return with a breaking news update...

HELP!
COSTUMES

CLICK

LD
FWOOOSH!

Squeee!

FLOOOP!

LD
FLip FLOP FLip FLOP
FLip FLOP FLip FLOP FLip FLOP FLip

Meanwhile...
Where are we goin', Papa?

We've gotta get out of town! I told you!!!

No, Papa! We gotta go back and save Sarah and Zuzu and Milly and Chief!!!

We **CAN'T!** We don't have any weapons!

All we've got is this measly old Shrink ray! It only has **Two Shots** Left!!!
But Papa-

Besides, I'm the BAD GUY! Everybody knows that!!!
But Papa-

I make poor decisions! I'm a SCOUNDREL!!!
But Papa-

I can't be goin' around being all Heroic and stuff...
But Papa-

...I've got a BAD REPUTATION to uphold!!!
But Papa-

If you only knew the horrible things I've done...

...the awful, un-forgivable things!!!

I'm just **EViL**, through and through.

That's all everybody expects from me.

You can Change, Papa.

Ya just gotta switch expectations!

Avoid Repetition... Uhhh... shum Redumbledorf...

ALRight, ALRight! I Get the Point!!!

But if I help your friends, then **<u>You've</u>** gotta do something for **<u>ME</u>**!

What?

but why?

Look — we've been through this a MILLION TIMES!

I AM NOT YOUR PAPA!

You're MY CLONE! There's A BIG DIFFERENCE!!!

oKay.

OKay **What?**

OKay,
Petey.

That's **BETTER!**
Now Let's go Save those Silly friends of Yours!!!

Meanwhile...
Stairs
FLOP FLIP FLOP FLIP FLOP FLIP FLOP FLIP

CLAP CLAP

RRRRRRRRR
Dog Man

RRRRRRRRR
DOG Man

RRR-
Dog MAN

THUNK!

DOG
Man

Meanwhile...
Petey--- oh, Peeeetey!!!

Come out and Plaaay-aaay!!!

Come out, come out, wherever you are!

Alright, kid. Listen up!

Here's the plan!

You stay here while I sneak out there...

... if I'm lucky, I'll be able to shrink those jerks...

...without hitting your friends!

Hey, Petey!
BONK

Did ya drop your shrink ray?
CHIEF
Well, well, well! Look who's here!!!

FIRE!!!
ZAP
KA-ZABBO
Hey, Petey! Knock-Knock!

ZAP!
KA-BLAM
Enough with the Knock-Knock Jokes! This is SERIOUS!
Aw, come on! This is the best one of my Life!
I SAID, NO!!!
BOOM
ZANG
You're just gonna make something poop on my head again!

I won't do that this time! C'mon---Knock-knock!
BAZONG
POW
ALRIGHT, Who's there?
Ummm...
ZING

ahhh...

a cloud...
A cloud, who?

A cloud pooped on your nose!

Ha Ha Ha Ha Ha Ha Ha Ha

I HAVE **HAD iT** with---
Ha Ha Ha Ha Ha Ha Ha

SLiP
Ha Ha Ha Ha Ha Ha

LI'L PETEY
Ha Ha Ha Ha Ha Ha Ha

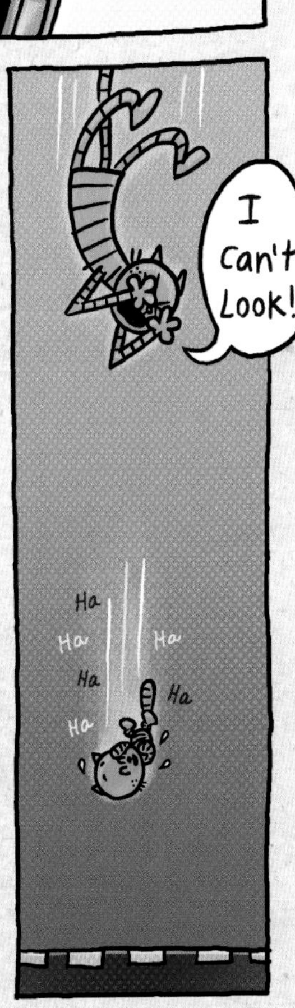
I can't Look!
Ha Ha Ha Ha Ha Ha

FOOSH
Oh, Hi Dog Man!
ZOOM

POONK
SCREEEECH!

Oops. I mean, Hi, The Bark Knight!

?

MY COSTUME!
COSTUMES

Let's Do This!

CHAPTER 6

SUPA BUDDIES

LD

Umm··· What are you guys doing?

We're practicing our superhero poses!

You know that the bad guys are here, right?
Yeah.

Hi, bad guys!!!

Hi!
Hi!

DON'T WAVE AT HIM! He's our ENEMY!

And any enemy of OURS shall soon be ANNIHILATED!

What do you have to say to THAT?

Knock-Knock!

Who's there?

Ummmm...

a airplane.

An airplane who?

A airplane pooped on your eyebrow!

Ha
Ha
Ha
Ha
Ha
Ha
Ha Ha
Ha
Ha
Ha

THAT'S NOT FUNNY!!!

Chief

So you like to Laugh, huh?

Well here's a funny story:

Once there were three evil villains...

...who built a giant Robo-Brontosaurus...

...That had a killer death ray!

Show 'em!!!

ZAP

CRASH

Hey, you were right!

That **WAS** a funny story!

Hey, The Bark Knight...

...now's our chance to save our friends!!!

Ready?

GO!
SWOOSH

shing
shing
CHIEF

SLICE
CHIEF

CHIEF
WE'RE FALLING!

Chief
We're STILL FALLING!

And I'm about to crash into the ground!!!

HOT DOG GLUE
Giant Left Sock
Sub-marine
Tuna Salad
Helicopter
"Weird Al" Music

Giant baseball GLOVE
Aardvark Repellent

chief
PLOOF!

chief

FLUP
Good catch, the Bark Knight!

But uh-oh!

We're about to crash into that factory!

brake
Gas
Quick! Step on the brake!

Boogie Fever
alphabet soup
Brake
Gas

SCREEECH

Welp, it looks like this is the end!
Yep! We're about to smash into that factory!
Chief
Rats!

Hey, it was nice knowing ya, Sarah.
Chief
Same here, Chief!!!

Good work, Milly!
Thanks, Chief! It was an honor to serve beside ya!

Bye-Bye, ZuZu. You were a good doggy!
Gee, I wonder what it will be like to not exist anymore.

Well, when you think about it...

None of us existed for trillions of years **BEFORE** we were born...

...And we didn't seem to mind it then!
Yeah--- I didn't even notice!!!!!
chief
True dat!

Let's not cry 'cuz we're Gonna die. Let's Laugh 'cuz we Got to **LIVE!!!**
Ha-Ha!
Yeah! Ha-Ha!
FACTORY

GIANT-MARSH-MALLOW FACTORY
KRACK
PLIP!
SMOOSH!
FLOOOP!
PLUH!

HeY! We didn't get Killed to death!!!
And we get to eat yummy marshmallows!
Win-win!!!

HeY, LOOK!!! It's our Heroes!

HOORAY FOR The SUPA Buddies!

Don't celebrate just yet...

...'cuz we're BAAAAACK!!!

It took forever, but we finally got ourselves out from under that building!!!

And NOW, we're gonna finish you ALL off...

...with ONE ZAP of our killer death ray!

So you'd better say "Goodbye!"

Bye-bye, Dog Man!
So Long, Sarah!
chief

Au revoir, Zuzu!
Adiós, Milly!
We love you, 80-HD!

WOULD YOU GUYS STOP BEING SO PLEASANT ABOUT EVERYTHING?!?

GO ON, ZAP 'em!

ZAP

Left hand here.

Right Thumb here.

Left hand here.

Right
Thumb
here.

Left hand here.

Right Thumb here.

That's my Papa!

I mean, that's Petey!

He's trying so hard to be good!

I always knew he had a good heart in there somewhere!
Chief

CHAPTER 7

The Darkness

Two hours Later...

PETEY!!!

CLONK

We've been battling for **HOURS**...

...And it hasn't gotten us **ANYWHERE**!!!

So I was thinking...

...Why are we fighting amongst **OURSELVES?**

If you and I set aside our differences...

... and we worked **TOGETHER...**

We'd be **UNSTOPPABLE!**

I mean, **REALLY...**

Think of the FUN we could have!!!

Think of the CASH we could swipe!

Think of the POWER we could wield!!!

Think of the CHAOS we could unleash!!!!!

Think of the DARKNESS we could inflict upon the unwashed masses!

Haven't you always wanted a sidekick?

A Partner in crime?

Isn't that why you created that dumb Little kitten in the first place?

Li'L Petey—
What a Wimp!

Hi—I'm Li'L Petey! Ooh—I'm so cute and Little and ever so GOOD!!!

HAW HAW HAW
HAW HAW
HAW
You can change, Papa.

Ya just gotta switch expectations!

So what do ya say, old buddy?

Let's ditch that obnoxious kid and go do some **crimes!**

DON'T TALK ABOUT MY SON THAT WAY!

Your **SON?**

I thought he was your **CLONE!**

Yeah, my **CLONE!** That's—that's what I meant.

Meanwhile...
CHIEF

Everyone was Transfixed by the drama above...
CHIEF

... When Suddenly...

AWESOME!

What?

I caught a fireFLy. Do ya wanna see it?

Fireflies give ya good Luck!

Let's go catch some more!!!

Meanwhile...
So--- you're gonna be a good guy now?
MAYbe I WiLL!

PBBBt! No WAY!!!

You can't change Your nature!!!

You're always gonna be a jerk just like me!

But hey, if you **REALLY** want to change **SO** much...

I've found just the thing!

Get ready for a **BIG** Change!

♫ Dum de dum de dum ♫

KLANK

SWOOOSH

CRASH

Oh, NO!!! Petey's in trouble! Let's GO!!

chief

chief

FLIP FLOP FLIP FLOP

Well, well, Well...

All of my Enemies Are together in ONE PLACE! How CONVENIENT!!!

OH, CRUNKY! OH, BUB!!!

CRUNKY! BUB!!!

Where did They GO???

BINOCULARS!

Those Two IDIoTS!

When I get my hooves on them---

WHAT ARE YOU TWO DOiNG?!!?

We're catchin' fireflies!

I WASN'T TALKing To YOU!!!

If you catch one, you get good luck!

I SAID I WASN'T TALKING TO YOU!

Hey, can you buy us a ice cream cone?

WHAT PART OF "I WASN'T TALKING TO YOU" DO YOU NOT UNDERSTAND?

Ummm...

... the middle part?

LET'S GO!!!
Why?

Because we've GOT WORK TO DO!
Why?

Because we're The BAD GUYS!
Why?

Because we've GOT ISSUES!
Why?

Because we have difficulty controlling our emotions!!!
Why?

Because we— HEY! I don't have to explain anything to you!!!
Why?

Because You're just A KiD!!!
Why?

WOULD YOU CUT THAT OUT???
Why?

Because I'm in Charge HERE!!!!!! YOU'RE NOT the BOSS OF ME!
Why?

BECAUSE YOU'RE NOT!!!

well maybe I Should be!

Who thinks I Should be the boss of Piggy?

Three against one. I win!

This is NOT A DEMOCRACY!

I-I can't believe you guys saved me!

We're the good guys, Petey!
That's what we do!
CHIEF

But...

...Where's the kid?

WHERE'S LI'L PETEY?

I'm up here, playin' with the bad guys!
CHIEF

RUFF RUFF
RUFF RUFF

RUFF
RUFF
RUFF

SWOOOOF

FLiiiiNG

80-HD!!!

We gotta save Dog Man!!!

Oops! I mean, **Lightning Dude!!!**

We gotta save **The Bark Knight!!!**

HURRY!!!

He's gonna crash into that building!!!

CRASH
CLOSED

Uh-oh...
SSSSSSSSSSSSSSSSSSSSS
CANNERY GROW
Closed
MAGIC GROWTH FORMULA
MAKES AnyThing Grow!

CANNERY GROW
MAGIC GROWTH FORMULA
MAKES ANYTHING GROW!
SMASH

GROW
CRASH

Ummmm...

Oops!

DOG MAN---
WAKE UP!!!

The Bad guys
Are Coming!!!

Well, well, well...
What do we have
here?

It Looks like you guys got yourselves in a big MESS!!!

Do you have any LAST WordS before we ZAP you all to SMiThereens?

Ummm...

...hmmm...

whisper whisper whisper

ZMMMMM

whisper whisper

VRRRR

zeeep

POP!

We'll tell ya our last word in a minute, ok?

MR. SQUIrTY's
SPrAY PAINT
FACTORY
Red Paint
Green Paint

OK, Strange flying cyborg kitten I've never met before. Take whatever you like!

Brown Paint
SO, You've returned. Are you ready To tell us your final word?
Almost!

Brown Paint
Brown Paint
ShaKA ShaKA ShaKA
OH, No! He's got Spray PAint!!!
CLOSE The hatch!!!
SSSSSSSSSSSSSSSS
Brown Paint

sSSSSSS
Brown Paint

sweeeet!

Now if I only had something to draw with...

oh!
Big ol' crayons

Perfect!

Let's see now...

OKay! I'm ready with my final Word!

Here it comes!

SQUiRREL!

Quadruple
FLIP-O-
Rama
Left
hand here.

Right Thumb here.

Good boy, Dog Man!
CRACKLE
CRUNCH
SLOBBER

chief

We missed Everything!!!
What happened?
Lick
Lick
Lick

WHere's The Kid??? Where's the Kid???
chief

WHERE is HE???

Knock
Knock

Left hand here.

Love, Sloppily

Love, Sloppily

Hey Papa, Look!

Dog Man Kissed us!

Yeeeeeeeeah...

...LoveLy.

HOORAY FOR DOG MAN!
...OOPS, WE MEAN
THE BARK KNIGHT!

CHAPTER 8

MY DOG MAN HAS FLEAS!

Well, I guess we—
hey, what's that?

What is it, Papa?

It's that Shrink ray I dropped back in chapter five.
Oh, yeah!

I wonder if it still works.
Let's find out!!!

ZAP

Yep. It worked!
Sweeeet!

Hey Gang! Petey saved the day!!!
Chief

HOORAY FOR PETEY!!!
Chief

OK, DOG Man,
Hand it over!!!
chief

Drop it!!!
chief

Seriously! Gimme the bad guys!!!
chief

C'mon, Dog Man! I have to take them to mini-Jail!
chief

LET GO!!!
chief

GiVE IT!!
chief

SNAP!

chief

chief

They're Gone!
chief

NOW LOOK WhAT YOU'VE DONE!!!
chief

The BAD GUYS GOT AWAY AGAin!
chief

I wonder where they went???
It sure is a mystery!
chief
scratch
scratch
scratch

Oh well, I have a feeling we'll never hear from them again!
chief
scratch
scratch

Something tells me the **SAME** thing!!!
chief
scratch
scratch
scratch

Well, c'mon Petey. It's time to go back to Jail!!!
Wait, what?
chief

I've gotta put ya back in Kitty custody!
chief

But I'm a good guy now!!!
chief
click

I know. But ya still gotta pay for the crimes ya did yesterday...
chief

...and the day before that, and the day before that, and the...
chief

Well That's Just GREAT!!!
chief
click

I WAS GOOD for, Like, THE WHOLE BOOK!
chief

AND IT DIDN'T MAKE ANY DIFFERENCE!
chief

Dog Man, I'm gonna go with them, okay?

Don't worry. Chief will walk me home.
scratch
scratch
scratch

G'night everybody! Let's all play again tomorrow!!!

Hey! WAit up!!!

chief

Are you sad, Papa?

NO! I'm MAD!!!
why?

Because it's just like when I was a Kid...

...Life is POINTLESS!!!
chief

If you're GOOD, Nobody CARES!!!

Ya gotta be good anyway, Papa!

If you're Kind, People just think you're WEAK!

Ya gotta be Kind anyway, Papa!

If you're HONEST, People just try to trick you!!!

Ya gotta be honest anyway, Papa.

If you're happy, People just get JEALOUS!
chief

Ya gotta be happy anyway, Papa!

You can spend YEARS creating stuff...

...Then a big robot brontosaurus can come along...

... and ZAP it all To SMIThereens in TWO SECONDS!!

Ya gotta be creative anyway, Papa.

Yeah, yeah, yeah! That's easy for **YOU** to say!

You're just a **kid**.

You don't know what a rotten, horrible place this world can be.
CHIEF

It can be so cold... so cruel...

... So unforgiving...

Papa...

...That's why we need to be good.

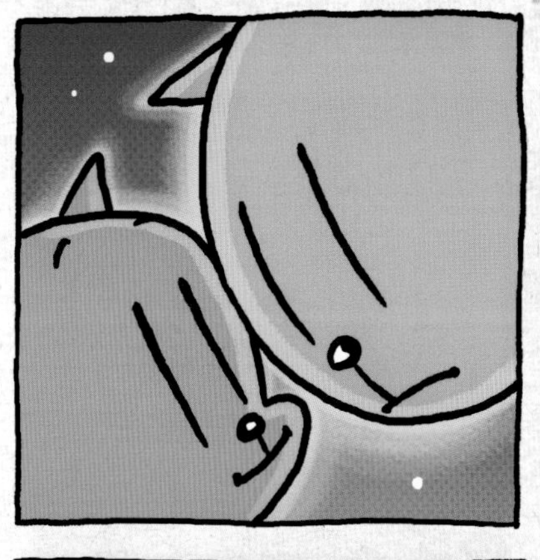

BWAAAWWW
You guys are So sweet!!!
Chief

MiND YOUR OWN BEESWAX, YA RUBBernecker!!!

Chief

Cat Jail

Hey Kid, Y'wanna get some gelato with me after I escape tomorrow?

I don't know what gelato is, but okay!

chief

chief

Hey Chief, what's gelato?
chief

It's Like ice cream.
Oh.
chief

chief
sweeeet!

The End

BUT WAIT...

...if you thought our adventure was over...
Dog Man

YOU AIN'T READ NOTHIN' YET!

Right now, George and Harold are busy reading ANOTHER old-fashioned book...
The Call of The WILD
Jack London
The Call of the WILD
Jack London

...getting AWESOME NEW-FASHIONED ideas...

... and desperately trying to figure out how to remove permanent marker from their faces before their moms find out!

So get ready for the next epic tale...

DOG MAN
BRAWL of The WiLD

If You Like THRiLLS...

...And you Like LAFFS...

...AND You Like AWESOMENESS...

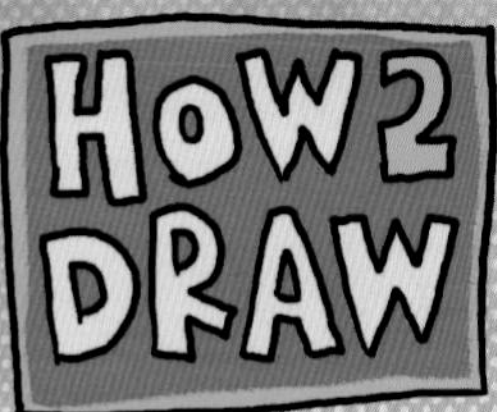

The BARK KNIGHT

in 42 Ridiculously easy steps!

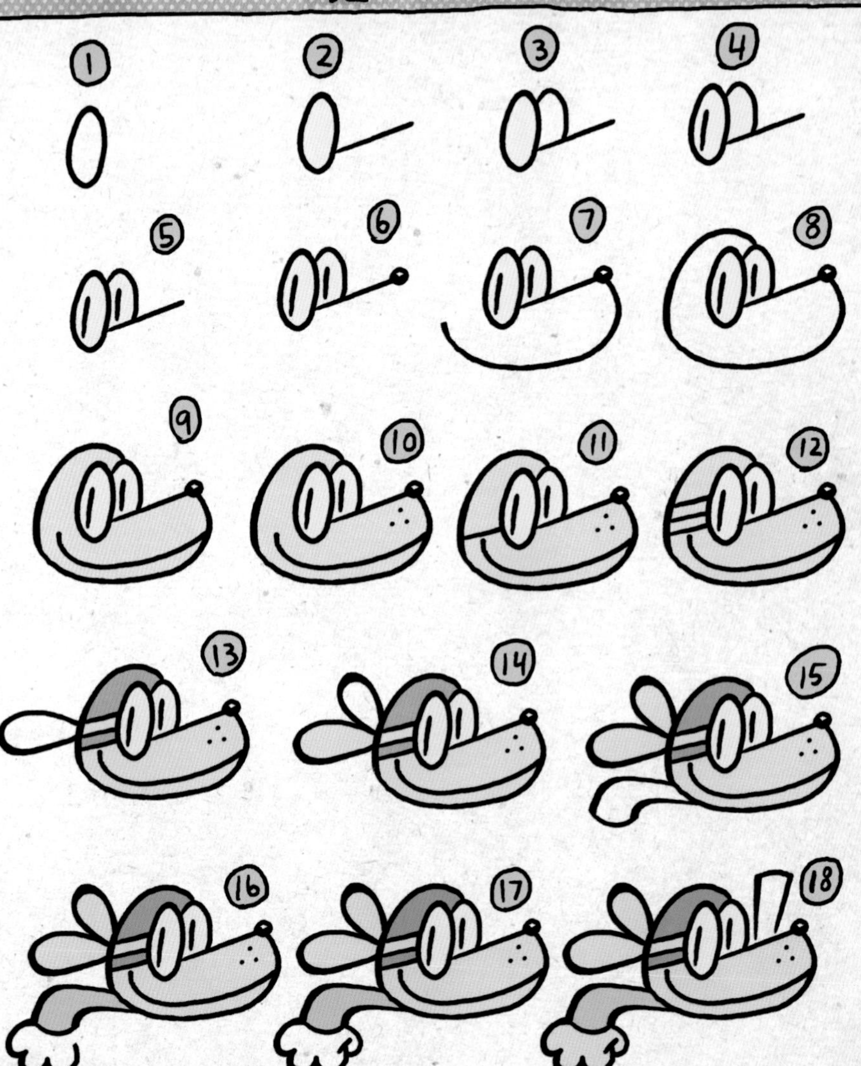

19
20
21
22
23
24
25
26
27
28
29
30
31
32
33

34
35
36
37
38
39
40
41
42

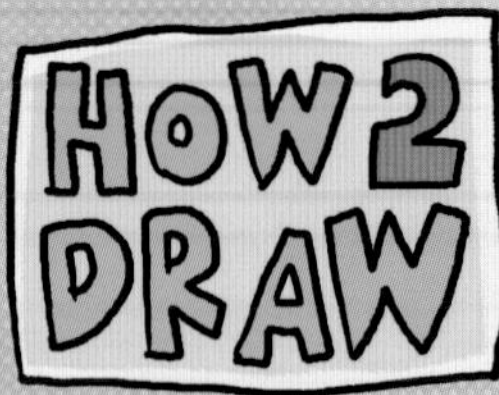

CAT KID

in 41 Ridiculously easy steps!

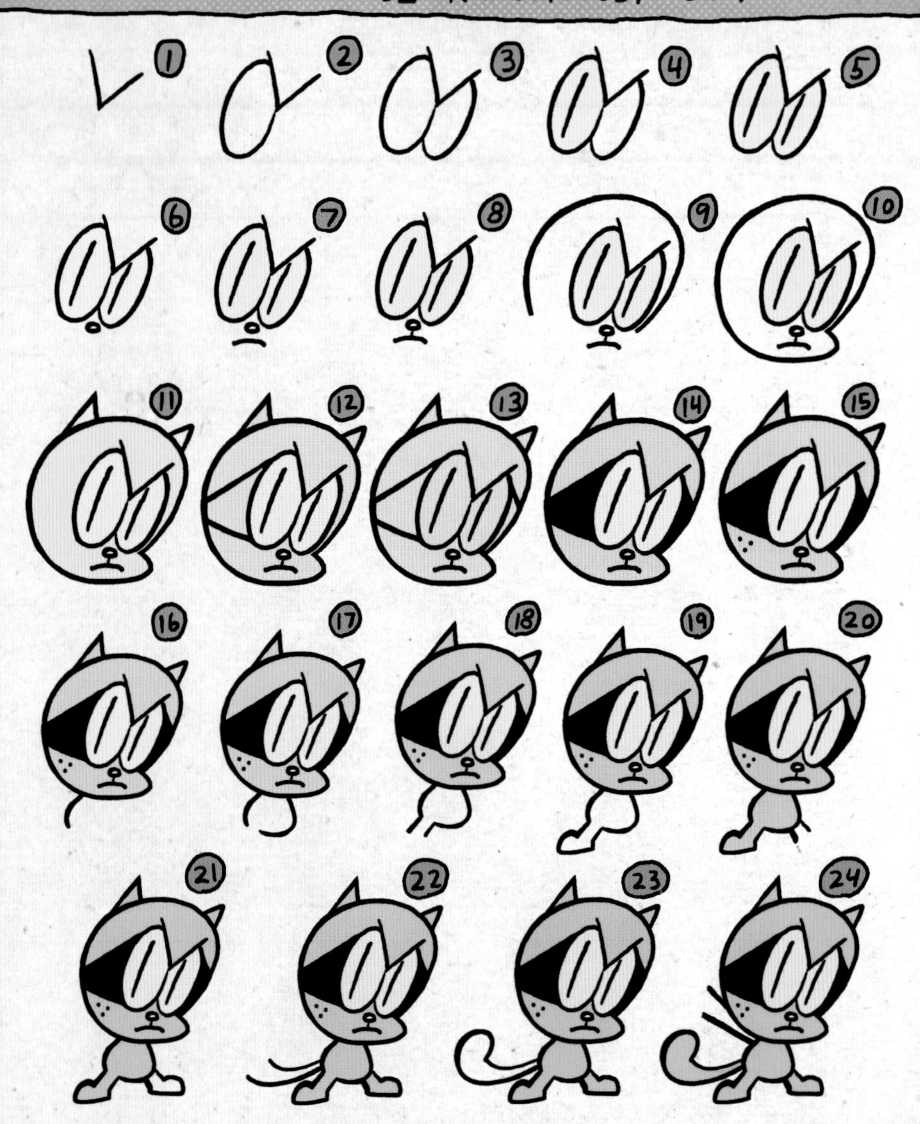

25
26
27
28
29
30
31
32
33
34
35
36
37
38
39
40
41

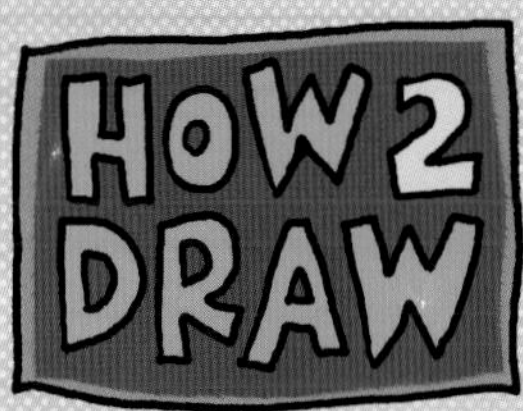

CRUNKY

in **26** Ridiculously easy steps!

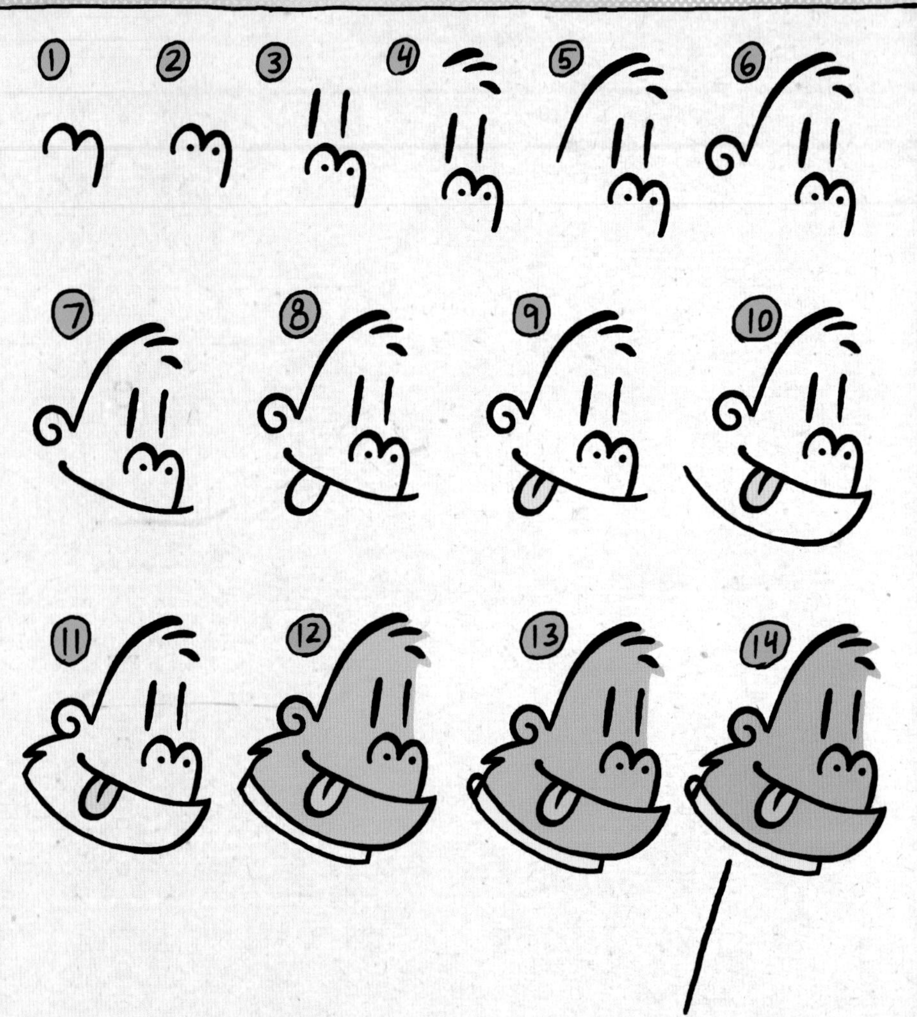

15
16
17
18
19
20
21
22
23
24
25
26

LIGHTNING DUDE

in **31** Ridiculously easy steps!

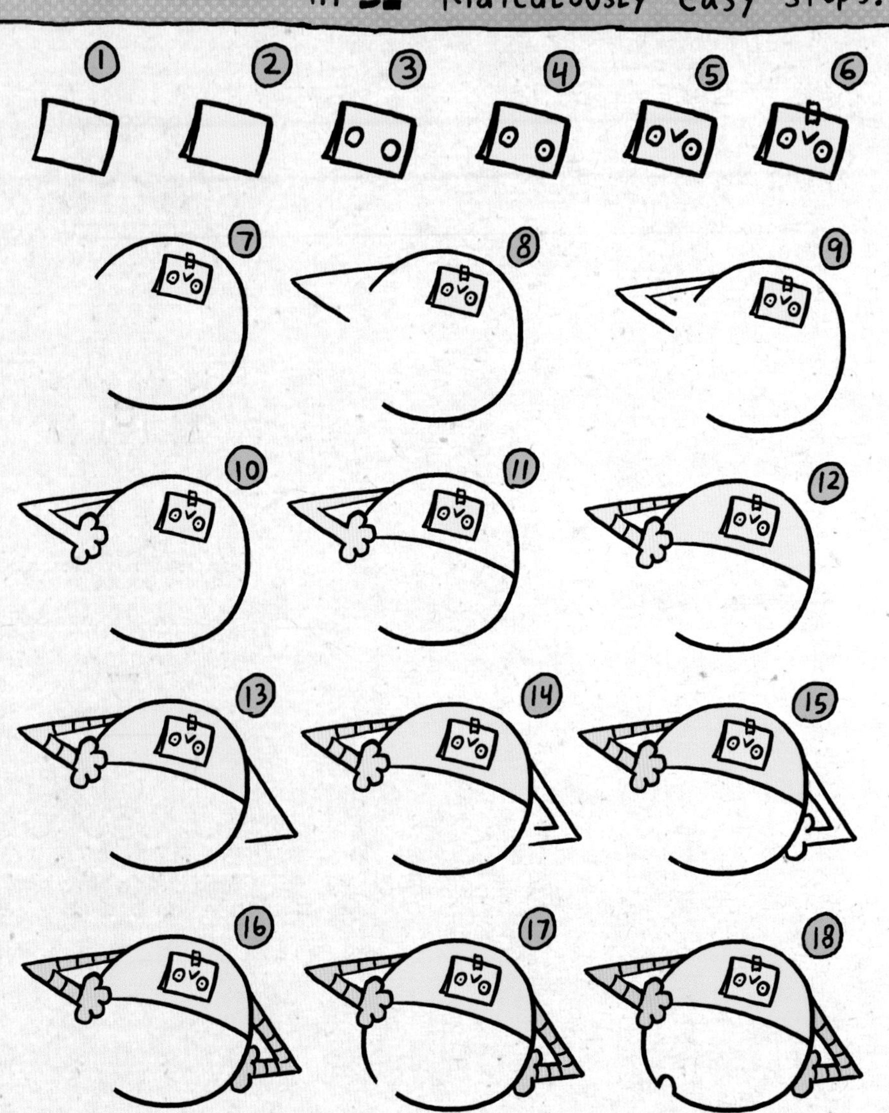

19
20
21
22
23
24
25
26
27
28
29
30
31

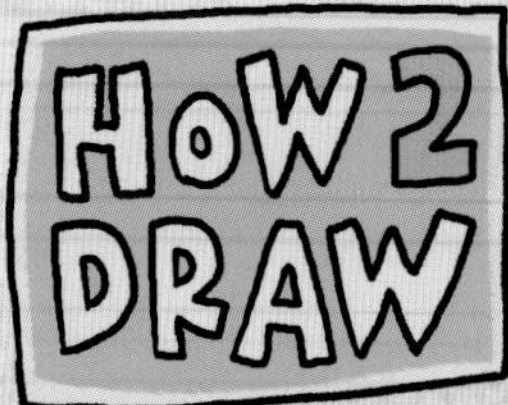

PIGGY

in 33 Ridiculously easy steps!

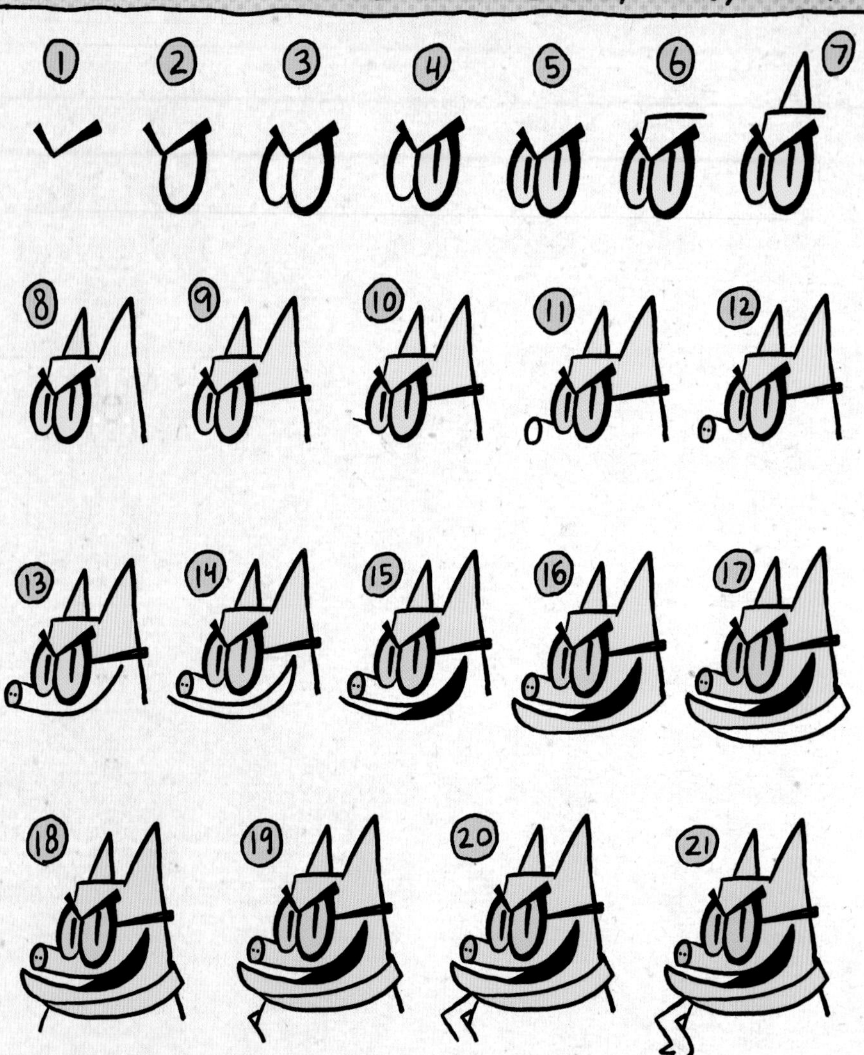

22
23
24
25
26
27
28
29
30
31
32
33

BUB

in **21** Ridiculously easy steps!

17
18
19
20
21

LEARN 2 DRAW MORE
STUFF!
at SCHOLASTIC.COM and
PILKEY.COM
chief

NOTES

by George and Harold

- ☆ Our favorite character from William Golding's Lord of the Flies is Piggy. The Piggy in our book is a bad guy, though.
- ☆ The dialogue on page 147 was inspired by quotes commonly attributed to Mark Twain and Dr. Seuss.
- ☆ The conversation on pages 220-221 was inspired by the poem "Anyway," by Kent M. Keith. A version of this poem is inscribed on the wall of Mother Teresa's home for children in Calcutta, India.
- ☆ "I finally finished reading Lord of the Flies. It WAS awesome." —Harold Hutchins

Read to Your CAT, Kid!

Studies* Show that Kids who read out loud to dogs...

* University of California-Davis: Reading to Rover, 2010

That's FAKE News!!!

it is?

Well, no— Probably not...

...but it's only HALF of the story!!

Experts believe that Kids can Get the SAME BeNeFiTS...

...by reading out Loud to CATS!!!
really?

Sure! Kids who read out loud to cats can improve their skills AND their confidence!!!
I'm getting better by the minute, Kid!!!
Me too, Kid!!!

They become better communicators, and participate more in class!
Yo! I got MAD COMMUNICATIN' SKILLZ, Kid!
Me too, Kid!!!

And they have reduced stress levels because cats don't judge 'em!
He accidentally skipped a word.
She didn't even notice.

* accompanied by a parent or guardian

...and the cats get the benefits of human interaction and socialization.

This helps make it easier for shelter cats to get adopted!

It's a **Win-Win** for everybody!

WOW! That's a great idea, Papa!

2 hours Later...
Cat Jail

Hey Petey! You've got a visitor!!!
I do?

Hey Kid. What'cha doing here?

I came to read to my cat, Kid!
Really?

check with your Local animal shelter and see if you can volunteer to **READ TO YOUR CAT, KID!**

READING TO YOUR CAT IS ALWAYS A PAWS-ITIVE EXPERIENCE!

SOPHIE & SKIPPY

MAUDE & MAX

MAUDE & ABBY

MAX & ALEX

CHARLIE & PAPOOSA

#ReadtoyourCatkid

AARON & PAPOOSA

JAC, KATE & DELILAH

KOUME, RINKA & YUMA

GALEN, FINN & RUCKUS

SOPHIA, ISABELLE, SCOOT & NINJA

LEARN MORE AT PILKEY.COM!

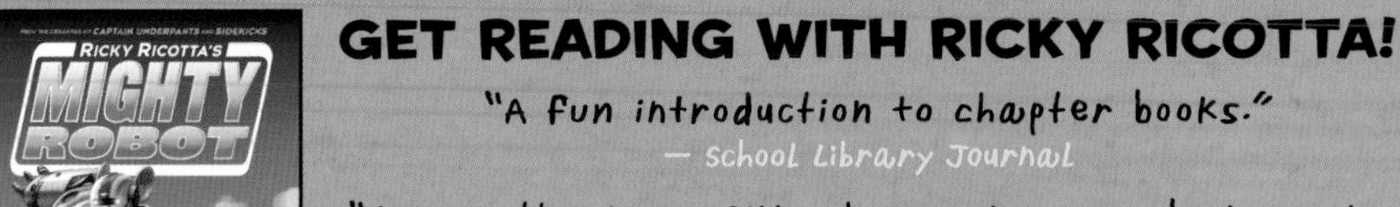

GET READING WITH RICKY RICOTTA!

"A fun introduction to chapter books."
— School Library Journal

"Has all the classic Pilkey hallmarks: comic book panels, superhero action, and Flip-O-Rama." — Booklist

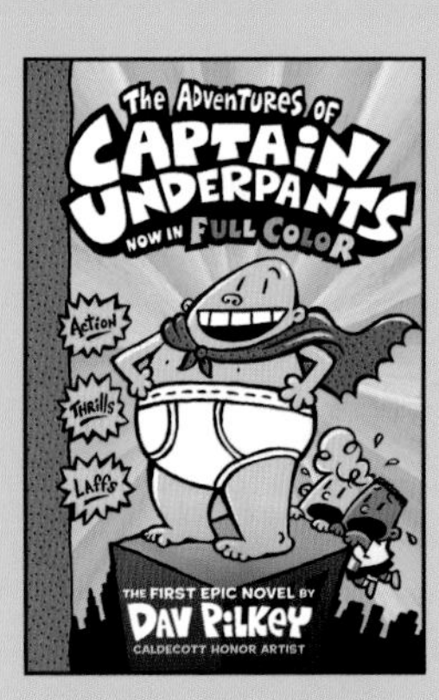

THE CRITICS ARE CRAZY ABOUT UNDERPANTS!

"Pilkey's sharp humor shines, and is as much fun for parents as their young readers." — Parents' Choice Foundation

"So appealing that youngsters won't notice that their vocabulary is stretching." — School Library Journal

KIDS ARE GAGA FOR GRAPHIC NOVELS!

"The laughs here (and there are many) are definitely spot-on for the intended audience."
— School Library Journal

"Will appeal to those who like silly adventures."
— Booklist

FANS ARE DIGGING THE TOP DOG!

★"Riotously funny and original."
— School Library Journal, starred review

★"An utter, unfettered delight."
— Booklist, starred review

★"Readers (of any age) will be giggling from start to finish."
— Publishers Weekly, starred review

PLANET PILKEY

Download the free Planet Pilkey app to start your digital adventure! Create an avatar, make your own comics, and more at planetpilkey.com!

ABOUT THE AUTHOR-ILLUSTRATOR

When Dav Pilkey was a kid, he suffered from ADHD, dyslexia, and behavioral problems. Dav was so disruptive in class that his teachers made him sit out in the hall every day. Luckily, Dav loved to draw and make up stories. He spent his time in the hallway creating his own original comic books.

In the second grade, Dav Pilkey created a comic book about a superhero named Captain Underpants. His teacher ripped it up and told him he couldn't spend the rest of his life making silly books.

Fortunately, Dav was not a very good listener.

ABOUT THE COLORIST

Jose Garibaldi grew up on the South Side of Chicago. As a kid, he was a daydreamer and a doodler, and now it's his full-time job to do both. Jose is a professional illustrator, painter, and cartoonist who has created work for Dark Horse Comics, Disney, Nickelodeon, MAD Magazine, and many more. He lives in Los Angeles, California, with his wife and their cats.